STORY TELLING FORTY THREE

Tides

Richard Seal

We are delighted to present Richard Seal's fourth book of verse, intriguing and thought-provoking poems about life.

Richard Seal's *'Tides'*

Tides

Published by

Percychatteybooks Publishing

ISBN 978 1 8381201 0 8

Copyright Richard Seal 2020

Richard Seal has inserted his right under the Copyright, Designs and Patents Act, 1988, to be identified as the author of this work.

All rights reserved

This book is sold subject to the condition that it shall not by way of trade or otherwise, be lent, resold, hired out, or otherwise circulated without the publishers' prior consent in any form of binding or cover other than that in which it is published and without a similar condition including this condition being imposed on the subsequent purchaser.

All characters and events in this publication are fictitious and any resemblance to any person living or dead is purely coincidental

STORY TELLING FORTY THREE   2

STORY TELLING FORTY THREE

Tides

Ever since my English teacher encouraged his class of twelve-year-old students to try writing a poem I have been hooked. Forty years on I remain grateful to the late Mr Langley.

This is my fourth collection of poetry following 'Wonders', 'Elements' and 'Strands'.

Richard Seal
24 July 2020

To R.F. Langley (1938 - 2011) ' .. as a cloud'.

Chapter One

Crayons

As Angie tidies her classroom
at the end of the afternoon,
she picks pieces of paper up,
left when the kids had had enough.
Remembers fondly sitting there
with pigtails in her long blond hair;
excitement of sticky fingers,
scent of pencil shavings linger.
Then, as now, coloured crayons look
tempting to eat. Picks up a book
with drawings by Emily;
adds one of her own - a pink tree.

☐

Bubble Gum

When standing in the pub alone,
checking messages on her phone,
a stranger at the bar approached,
and she stepped back as he encroached
briefly on her personal space.
The man said sorry, looked shamefaced;
but when he spoke a few soft words,
defences dropped and it occurred
to the woman that he might be
the boy who kissed her by the tree
a lifetime ago when at school.
The girl had giggled, felt a fool,
then ran away and left him there
with red flushed cheeks and tousled hair.
Eyes reveal, as she is struck dumb,
he might still taste of bubble gum.

Free

The girl holding the bridle, clad
in breeches and jodhpurs, feels sad,
wracked with doubt, unable to shake
fear and stress which keeps her awake.
Horse walks, steadfast in gracefulness;
sun-dappled, he is never less
than a creature of dignity.
Beautiful, majestic and free.

Stored

The storage unit has long stood
undisturbed, abandoned for good
on the day ten years' fee was paid
by a young man who looked afraid.
Manager would never have guessed
he would leave false name and address.
Man could not leave quickly enough,
keen to turn his back on the stuff.
Heavily wrapped, deep in one box
under dusty books, an old clock
and an egg-timer lacking sand
lay his rival's severed right hand.

Number Two

Lisa feels happy to be boss
in all but name - she feels no loss,
operating as number two.
Always does what she wants to do,
content to let manager take
credit for her ideas, mistakes.
When any staff disputes occur,
it is nothing to do with her.
As master manipulator,
her coup de grâce will come later.
The woman, more than anything,
takes pleasure in pulling the strings.

Richard Seal's *'Tides'*

Died young, but living
each day at full tilt secured
immortality.

Since mum passed away,
cradling her teacup, fingers
curled now means the world.

Huge tumour cannot
be removed; no grief, she prays
torment will be brief.

The first voice was nice,
sadly being put through leads
to red blotch fury.

Adviser

Adviser works at home a lot
these days, has online meeting slots
for clients in her office space,
much easier than face-to-face.
Likes no longer having to drive
for hours. She has seen business thrive;
seems to get busier each day,
working in a much smarter way.
Video calls are all the rage,
but Janette is often upstaged
by tabby cat washing himself
behind her, comfy on a shelf;
from the vantage point of his bed,
hears her advice, then shakes his head.

Reattached

Retina is reattached, held
in place by a band - hard to tell
just yet if the operation
has resolved the situation.
Although surgeon predicts poor sight,
Tim's vision is up for a fight;
it battles through bloodshot and blur
to make a miracle occur.
While man bides his time, needs to wait,
eyes agitate to calibrate.

Mounds

Walking on the uneven ground
in the churchyard, there is no sound
to be heard, yet the friends concede
there might be movements in the trees.
From behind a crypt they expect
a spectre to appear; detect
amid piles of dust and bones
a uniqueness beneath stones .
Lads know if they open their minds
they might find spirits that are kind;
ghosts who had happy lives, not cursed.
From beyond, faint echoes of mirth.
But coming across nameless mounds,
neither boy wants to stick around.

Carousel

This seasoned traveller knows well
that she faces the carousel
of lookalike luggage; standing
beside passengers demanding
their belongings back straight away.
Smiles to herself, makes Zoe's day
when she sees furious faces
at their badly battered cases.
Missing locks and big dents cause moans
which tickle Zoe's funny bone.

Group Call

Cannot abide online phone calls
with groups of people. Feels appalled
at the sight of beaming faces
in their separate split screen places.
The man glowers in his tight box,
seldom speaking as he takes stock
of the boredom lodged in his brain.
Next time he is going to abstain,
this process goes beyond the pail;
from now on he will send emails.

Sunglasses

Like his favourite celebrities,
Brad tries his best to look at ease
wearing his sunglasses indoors;
but grim Grimsby does not afford
the same bright weather as LA.
This lad lacking tan has to stay
alert to avoid rain showers.
While glitterati have the power
to make hotel staff open doors,
the Englishman is just ignored
when checking in with plastic bags;
he might as well be wearing rags.
Nobody seems to be aware
of this teenage millionaire.

Midnight Feast

The lad enjoyed a midnight feast;
exhilaration was released
when the family was asleep
and it was safe for him to creep

down the stairs in the dead of night.
In the fridge he thrilled at the sight
of mystery things wrapped in foil
or frozen so they would not spoil.

He helped himself to chicken legs
with hunks of cheese and boiled eggs.
But the magic stopped when a note
left by mum asked what he liked most.

Thirst

Sits staring with unfocused eyes
at the gin and tonic; she tries
to think back to having the first,
before developing a thirst
which is unlikely to be quenched.
While dependency is entrenched,
has no desire to lose her crutch;
she loves the drink's effects so much.
Could ditch the ice and lemon slice -
the bottle alone would suffice.

Richard Seal's *'Tides'*

As an adult, finds play
park shrunken, views foreshortened,
boundaries pulled tight.

His hide-and-seek tree
still stands in the park, a cross
painted on its stump.

Atop Empire State
cowers, struggles to resist
urge to scale the fence.

He feels like pale blue
compared to her red, Spring dew
to blazing July.

Road Trip

When her human servants moved house,
Jemima the cat missed one mouse
who had managed to get away
from her clutches on the last day.

As unfinished business annoyed
the feline greatly, she employed
her focus and intelligence
on strategy - a plan commenced.

One Sunday evening after dark
the fearless Jemima embarked
with resolve on a long long trip,
taking nothing more than cat nip.

She kept to minor roads and lanes
where possible, tried to refrain
from crossing many motorways,
but did it twice and was not phased.

A greater test was a river,
but her wit and guile delivered.
By tying branches, twigs with reeds,
the cat's boat was bound to succeed.

Richard Seal's *'Tides'*

After fifty miles she got tired,
but Jemima then felt inspired.
Hitched a welcome ride on a bus,
the driver did not make a fuss.

When close to her destination,
she assessed the situation;
relaxed on an old neighbour's lap,
being fed very well by the chap.

After eighty miles on the road
cat prepared to lighten her load.
Now back at her previous home
she left the new doggie alone

and paid no attention at all
to the two boys playing football.
She headed into undergrowth
to find the mouse she wanted most.

Achieved her mission at a stroke,
the sense of failure was revoked.
She licked all her paws, felt okay;
had a snooze then went on her way.

Matched

The online dating service said
that Caroline's profile matched Dean's
therefore, the couple went ahead
and arranged a date - both were keen.

She arrived at the cafe first,
and sat at a table outside;
spotting the man, she feared the worst
and panicked with nowhere to hide.

Supposedly thirty, he seemed
to be ten years older than that;
While the tubby, balding man beamed
Caroline was left feeling flat.

Dean wished that the sweating would stop,
Excitement refused to abate;
determined not to be a flop,
he wanted to impress his date.

The man thought she seemed really nice,
so friendly with lovely blue eyes;
would she like the curry and rice
or opt for the homemade steak pie?

When he ordered she shook her head
and asked for salad no dressing;
he had large breakfast with fried bread,
saying with a grin 'No messing!"

Richard Seal's *'Tides'*

Dean asked about Caroline's work,
she talked about being a cook;
he said teaching was great for perks:
free paper, pens, exercise books.

The woman was a bit surprised
that Dean was so funny and warm;
he listened and seemed to be wise;
Caroline's impressions reformed.

Discussing culture they had larks:
the woman said she did not find
Karl as funny as Groucho Marx.
When he laughed she had to remind

her companion, convulsed with mirth,
that what he had said was untrue:
the Pope, in fact, has been since birth
a Catholic and not a Jew.

Dean quickly struck to get her back
by explaining that Stevie Smith
could only have been in Fleetwood Mac
if she had given poems a miss.

When they parted, both felt relaxed,
Caroline's defences were down;
with all her prejudices axed,
she knew a good match had been found.

Eye of the Storm

Rachel spent three months with her head
in chaos, while excitement spread
to cause constant stomach churning,
emotion stoked up and burning.
It felt like a white knuckle trip
as raw emotions surged and gripped.
Then her boyfriend's car hit a tree,
he was dead when they cut him free.
Alone in the eye of the storm,
Rachel's life lost all meaning and form;
Diminished in despair and doubt,
her whirlwind had blown itself out.

On The Severn

Boating on the river Severn,
is a tranquil peace of heaven,
avoiding swans and fishing lines
and hoping that the day stays fine.
Just as some kingfishers are seen
the pair hit problems unforeseen.
When the man foolishly rises,
the boat rocks and then capsizes.
Plans for a perfect day implode,
no picnic now at Hampton Loade.

Black and White

Camera favours black and white,
subtleties of darkness or light
captured expertly by her lens.
The sharpness of focus depends
on whether sunshine is aflame
or shadows infiltrate her frame.
The presence of bright colours mar
a classic montage of film noir.

Wicket

The Englishmen in Spain loves sport,
but the situation is fraught
because Jack does not like football,
or tennis or handball at all.
Volleyball with friends on the beach
is absolutely out of reach,
and water-sport of any kind
could not be further from his mind.
When he suggests a rugby game
it clearly goes against the grain,
while crown green bowling or cricket
leave him on a sticky wicket.
In the end, back in the saddle,
friends persuade him to try Padel.

Housemate

Barry recognises the face
and voice of the ageing barman;
instantly returns to that place
where life as a student began.

The housemates were like chalk and cheese:
Dave loved the pub, and always mocked
Barry the film fan; as a wheeze
defaced his posters. Deeply shocked

at this behaviour, things got worse
for Barry, who was derided
for talking too posh while his verse
was ridiculed. He decided

in the end he had to move out.
Feeling broken, never knew why
the sustained abuse came about
while the others turned a blind eye.

Pain still lingers thirty years on;
Dave offers an uncertain grin
Although relieved hatred has gone,
Barry cannot smile back at him.

Plan

Always felt like the odd one out,
classmates left Phillp in no doubt
that he was useless at football,
in fact, good at no sport at all.
Girls showed no interest in the lad
yet Phil never seemed to be sad
that he only had one true friend:
an even odder kid called Len.
No one knew of the pair's grand plan
to send everyone down the pan.
They got one over on the class
though the scheme never came to pass.

Short

Max was a head and shoulders short
of most of the students he taught.
He had been small all of his life,
nowhere near as tall as his wife.
His children looked down on their dad,
but this never made him feel bad.
Everyone could tell at first sight
What the man plainly lacked in height
he made up for in his great weight
which increased at a steady state.
Max had no problem being fat,
it was something he excelled at.

Richard Seal's *'Tides'*

Tortoise pulls his head
back into his shell, will try
again next decade.

Deep in the mountains
forgotten cave house conceals
a three-legged chair.

Tried to reach the sun
on his best friend's trampoline.
Caught a butterfly.

Frozen to the spot
dog needs to pass sleeping cat;
twitch signals intent.

Foot in Mouth

Her boyfriend made her roll her eyes
so many times, Jan could not count;
attempts at humour were unwise,
folk offended began to mount.

His own worst enemy for sure,
had a rush of blood to the head:
With timing impeccably poor,
the wrong thing would always be said.

Although Billy meant no harm
when putting his foot in his mouth,
Jan would bite her lip in alarm
every time a night out went south.

Class

Class 2A seldom settled down
regardless of their teacher's frowns.
Alongside chat, streams of giggles
there were a fair share of niggles:
a ruler leant but not returned,
imagined slights, former friend spurned.
But sad news left the class bereft;
after Christmas Miss Jones had left.

Violinist

Christina loved her violin.
Her practice sessions would begin
each summer evening at midnight;
seemed oblivious to the sight
of neighbours slamming windows shut.
Played instinctively from the gut;
unaware people, dogs and cats
and even the neighbourhood rats
were now leaving hand over fist
to escape this violinist.
All forms of life had had enough,
even flies and moths wore earmuffs.

Bouncer

Although Vince had a job at last
felt it was unlikely to last
longer than a couple of shifts.
The young man did not have a gift
for being a doorman with steel.
This kindly bouncer did not feel
inclined to turn punters away;
he smiled and passed the time of day.
While never being rough or tough,
the man seemed to have the right stuff;
stopped trouble before it arrived.
The gentle custodian thrived.

Chapter Two

Agua Con Gas

His señorita served him here
time after time when he appeared
to order water and a snack.
John had to keep on coming back
and overcome shyness and fear
in order to see Lucia.
Looking at his fiancée now,
the man can finally see how
his falling in love came to pass:
she had him at agua con gas.

Young Master

Master Woofter, a young canine
of good breeding, was kept in line
and well clear of disputes and spats
by a very special black cat.

Johnson was both shrewd and refined;
this feline's personal feline
had left all his colleagues agog
when he went to work with a dog.

Had the finest valet gone mad?
Although the young master was glad
to have this marvel cat on board,
the dog's instructions were ignored

if they did not suit the valet.
The feline had a lot to say
about attire and etiquette,
his high standards had to be met.

Any clothes master selected
were scrupulously inspected;
even if Woofter insisted,
Johnson usually resisted.

With will of iron, the valet steered
a course whereby scarves disappeared;
if a new hat was not approved
it would rapidly be removed.

Richard Seal's *'Tides'*

The coat selection would not do,
while Johnson threw out half the shoes;
sports jackets were given away
before Woofter could have a say.

Trips to his nefarious club
were discontinued, Binky snubbed;
Bunkers was uncouth to the core
so was turned away at the door.

Only Cuthbert survived the cut,
his trousers were appropriate;
dining companions were vetted,
and young master was indebted

to top cat for helping him see
the way through high society.
Woofter's gaffes and blunders got less,
but how could the hapless dog guess

Johnson's plans to give, with stricture
his successor the full picture;
he had to let him know the score,
understand what he was in for.

But in the end Johnson softened,
which had not happened too often.
When the cat left the dog's employ,
spoke fondly about the dear boy.

Richard Seal's *'Tides'*

The marble-cool crypt,
so tranquil in the sunshine
offers sanctuary.

Embraces the stars,
enlisting constellations
to shoot for the moon.

Stares up at the fan
rotating on the ceiling.
Mosquitoes stand down.

Sits alone in Church,
petrified by shock of loss,
believing nothing.

Catchphrase

Colleagues often go through a phase
of trying to use a catchphrase.
Micky employs "I have a weight
problem to keep up here, workmates"
Fran says her sister gets her down:
"We get on like a house burnt down!"
For Fred "Some need help, you can tell,
to get right back inside their shell."
Boss has been trying for a while
to think of a phrase with some style
that she could reel off with a smirk
to urge them to get down to work.

Bones

When grandson comes in with some bones
he has unearthed, Joyce does not moan
that he has dug up her garden;
being careful not to harden
her tone of voice, asks lad to keep
clear of where dogs in heaven sleep.
She takes his spade to make him stop,
then sends Timmy off to the shops
to buy some sweets. Hopes he forgets
what he found, would be more upset
about what else is in the ground
if she let him dig further down.

Procession

While Southern European pine trees
are striking, they make people freeze
at the thought of chilling killer
processionary caterpillars.

Biding their time in fluffy nests,
creatures join forces in a quest
to march in columns, soldier on
until all resistance has gone.

If by chance they touch human hair,
the follicles will not return there;
cause rashes, skin irritation,
such a stressful situation.

In general, cats will stay away
in favour of less toxic prey;
give them a wide berth, seem aware
of the dangerous body hair.

However, hapless dogs might lick
the caterpillars then get sick.
Necrotic tongues are hard to take,
such an agonising mistake.

Pipe Dreams

Loved to hold forth over his tea
pontificating pompously
from the comfort of his armchair;
he felt like King of the World there.
With remote control in his hand
all the dogs seemed to understand
he was, without question, the boss.
His wife looked at George, at a loss.
Anne had tried to help realise
the man's goals but this was unwise:
preferred to do nothing, it seemed,
let hot air inflate his pipe dreams.

Toilet Bowl

Woman fell to her knees to clasp
the toilet bowl; ceramic grasped
in desperation as the beer
mixed with lots of wine re-appeared;
Her stomach, violently lurching
seemed to delight in the burning
sensation of molten-chunked death
accompanied by rank bad breath.
Brief respite before final push
to evacuation then flush.

Flatline

Man had always been a nightmare,
moaning that life was so unfair;
he railed against imagined slights,
and took truculence to new heights.
However, when he passed away
colleagues found some nice things to say.
Rough edges slowly became smoothed,
harsh memories of turbulence soothed;
folk concluded that he was good
deep down, but so misunderstood.
Though smiles were not seen on his face,
the man's heart was in the right place.
All is forgiven, things are fine
when a person has reached flatline.

Fancy

Waking from her slumber, Nancy
always does what takes her fancy.
The feline can take all the time
in the World to plan her next crime.
For now feels content in repose;
the Persian cat wrinkles her nose
in dead of night or break of day,
she checks her pads and slinks away.

Red

A few months after they had wed
Linda sensed an impending dread.
Paul's sense of humour disappeared,
his smile mutated to a sneer;
Enjoyed having his wife around
to delight in putting her down.
The spitefulness just fuelled the hate
chipped away at her mental state.

Lynne increasingly fantasised
about bringing Paul down to size,
then one day snapped, saw crimson red
threw a glass ashtray at his head.
Felt calm as she saw blood spurting
up the walls and on the skirting.
As her husband slumped to the floor
she did not feel scared any more.

Roast Dinner

Englishman in Spain takes a seat
in a British pub for a treat:
wants to relish a Sunday roast.
As a child he loved beef the most.
Yorkshire pud would go down a storm,
but now he finds he feels lukewarm
about roast potatoes and sprouts.
Without a shadow of a doubt,
he prefers paella, tapas:
gambas y patatas bravas.

White Star

The Unsinkable Ship went down
in 1912, and two thirds drowned.
Titanic did not have enough
lifeboat seats, so men were rebuffed.

Just a few needed restraining,
most stood back without complaining.
The ship's band continued to play,
none of them tried to get away.

While first class passengers fared well,
some in third class were sent to hell,
with many kept locked behind gates
to meet an unspeakable fate.

Officer Lightoller survived
to see his hero status thrive -
The main man on an upturned boat,
he kept the freezing crew afloat.

The Chairman of the White Star Line
claimed a free place, and just in time.
With fifteen hundred people lost,
this man was left to count the cost.

With Captain gone, Ismay was blamed,
a scapegoat for collective shame.
This broken man with honour stripped
should have gone down with the ship.

Unfair

Travelling in the car was no joke
as a child, Anne's parents chain-smoked
but refused to open a window.
She wondered how they did not know
it was horrible and unfair
to stop her from breathing fresh air.
She grew up shunning cigarettes
to protect her children, and yet
never hesitates to curse
at drivers; blows horn, getting worse.
Does not see hands covering ears
as her daughters cower in fear.

One Liner

Long, rambling jokes leave Ian cold,
feeling bored, they are always told
by people a little too fond
of their own voice. Tends to respond
with a fixed smile when the punchline
or delivery fails to shine.
The man is also uninspired
by most puns - they always seem tired.
Whilst a one-liner is the best,
and pithy asides can impress,
funniest thing of all for him:
slipping on a banana skin.

Virus

Computer virus takes pleasure
creeping in at its own leisure
to take root in your attachments,
attack with no chance of defence.
Causes havoc with dirty tricks
designed to leave you feeling sick.

When the computer has been cleaned,
be on your guard - this does not mean
that the virus, now retreated,
has been completely defeated.
It may bide its time, sitting tight,
lurk behind a recipe site.

Moment

Sat together on the settee,
semi-focused on the TV,
the pair were joking and flirting,
smiling and laughing while skirting
around elephant in the room.
Sensing something might happen soon,
the couple lapsed into silence,
and the atmosphere became tense.
A relationship which simmered
for ages suddenly glimmered
as her hand rested on his knee;
he reciprocated, both felt free
as feelings, which had grown and thrived,
blossomed; the moment had arrived.

Richard Seal's *'Tides'*

Granny, at the end
showed in pleading eyes battle,
long fought, was over.

As the clocks go back,
chill grips with deep depression.
Isobars close in.

Man on the highway
is tyre-branded, nose askew;
eyes gaze way beyond.

Tone heavy, laden
with sarcasm lightened by
gentle words dissolved.

Plough On

The woman's workload is so tough,
twenty four hours are not enough.
Makes a coffee, drinks half a cup
drops off in her chair then wakes up
to spittle round her mouth gone dry,
and large black bags under her eyes.
Checks her watch, it is now too late
to go out for drinks with her mates.
Grits her teeth and ploughs on instead,
too tired to take herself to bed.

Thyroid

After years not feeling inspired
by very much, sluggish and tired,
the man suddenly feels relieved
with the diagnosis received:
an under active thyroid gland
is not so hard to understand.
Taking just one tablet a day,
he feels much better, seems okay
to eat pies and curry, drink beer
now this great excuse has appeared.
Cannot be blamed for being fat,
medical condition caused that.

Purple

The woman had loved luscious shades
of crimson, violet; often made
fresh lilac or lily displays;
but her darkness deepened each day
and demons encroached when alone.
When she did not answer the phone

shocked neighbours found crocuses crushed
and a broken vase; voices hushed.
Hanging with skirts in purple prints
and fine dresses in flowered chintz
Zoe was dead in an alcove
with neck furrows and face turned mauve.

Prang

New car stalls, fluffy dice collide,
Rachel is left shocked and wide-eyed
at the sickening sensation
of crunch and jolt. Agitation
escalating as she climbs out,
the woman expects to hear shouts
and expletives, but man is tame,
says sorry, accepts the full blame
for pranging her yellow Mustang.

Soft Drink

Barman Andy saw many come
and go over the years, had fun
identifying customers
by their drinks. The man got a buzz
predicting who would be bitter,
wine or vodka; had a titter
to himself when he got caught out:
snowball for him, for her a stout.
For some reason drinkers of mild
were seldom seen cracking a smile,
while it always struck him as weird
that most Guinness drinkers had beards.

He did not ask why 'double gin'
switched to juice, became very thin
and looked worse and worse every day;
later heard that she had passed away.
Despite his verdict, Geordie Pete
said he would not accept defeat,
wanted his friends to understand
he would die with pint glass in hand.
Andy was known to like real ale,
though, in fact, this was a tall tale.
Was not sure what people would think
if they knew he preferred soft drinks.

Marilyn

A timeless icon people feel they know
through her acting, beauty, luminosity
is movie actress Marilyn Monroe,
whose private life was often all at sea.

The audience laughed at 'Seven Year Itch'
'Monkey Business', 'Gentlemen Prefer Blondes';
In 'The Prince and the Showgirl' she bewitched
and the audience would always respond.

Haunting 'Misfits' concluded her career,
she had given everything she had got.
However, her image won't disappear,
'nobody's perfect' in 'Some Like It Hot'.

At thirty six finally crashed and burned,
headed down a 'River of No Return'.

Blank

Frustrated and perplexed, she stares
down at the blank page, feels aware
this may well be a fruitless night.
Often flails, unable to write
inspiring stories, and her verse
with its tired rhymes, is getting worse.
While she soldiers on, with a need
to be creative and succeed,
her muse is fading, losing heart,
preparing the ground to depart.

Richard Seal's *'Tides'*

Sal dwells on friendship
not sought. New couple drop by
to darken doorstep.

In Brittany heat
over forty, wants to strip
off flesh to the bone.

From box in the loft
beige jumper and yellow flares
sheepishly emerge.

Beleaguered train guard
bears curses until tunnel.
Lashes out in dark.

Trunk

The trunk was Jenny's private place;
her sisters dared not show their face
when she wanted to look inside.
The only time one of them tried
to take a peek, she was so scared
when swung round the room by her hair.

On leaving home, the trunk came too.
The young woman turned the air blue
when a foolish friend tried the lock;
he turned and fled, speechless with shock.
Her suitors were dropped like a stone
if they did not leave it alone.

For the rest of Jenny's long life
she avoided trouble and strife
with trunk hidden safely away.
Opened in secret, did not say
anything to her family
about things not for them to see.

Only after the woman died
did her husband and sons decide
it would be okay to find out
just what all the fuss was about.
However, no one was prepared
to find there was nothing in there.

Richard Seal's *'Tides'*

Bright

A lot of people call Kate 'bright'
because of her high marks at school;
the girl does homework every night
and she studies hard as a rule.

However, Kate is far from keen
to be seen as run of the mill.
She is not just a normal teen,
behind pale blue eyes lies a chill.

Frost has permeated since birth:
An ice sculpture exists inside.
The girl's deep freeze is getting worse
and becoming harder to hide.

Knitter

Beetle felt quite pleased with himself.
Aside from being in good health,
he loved to scuttle over roots
then nibbling stems and new shoots.
He lived between two massive rocks,
under leaves, where he darned his socks
and knitted jumpers for his friends.
Admirers started to descend,
so to satisfy the masses
beetle gave some sewing classes;
for the price of just a few seeds
he helped other insects succeed.

Chapter Three

Pictures

All her life Priscilla has found
that the wind and rain contain sounds
which touch her on a different plane,
in ways that she cannot explain.

She also sees pictures in flames,
rocks and clouds, and gives them all names;
shifting shapes appear in her dreams
which are never quite what they seem.

Growing older, feels delighted,
sense of wonder still ignited.
Looking at paintings, discovers
elusive spectres uncovered.

□

Jokers

His colleague liked a belly laugh,
seemed more than happy to be daft.
The couple's banter reached new heights
when they worked together on nights.

She sometimes found it hard to stay
focused when her friend was at play.
They larked around and had a ball,
neglecting duties, missing calls.

The pair continued for a while
to flirt with each other and smile.
There was not much to laugh about
when the jokers were weeded out.

Covered

Marcus always jumps out of bed
at the crack of dawn, restless head
full of 'to do' lists and new plans;
his wife Gill can not understand
how the man can get up and go
when she just does not want to know
until nine at the earliest.
But then the woman will insist
on late nights, still cooking on gas
long after his bedtime has passed.
Between them, pair have discovered,
twenty four hours are covered.

U-Turn

Belinda's husband seems to be
an absolute authority
on every topic known to man.
Roger's knowledge appears to span
science and nature, history, art,
politics too; he knows by heart
all the facts and can reel them off
at will. It is unwise to scoff
or argue with dogmatic views,
though his wife is always amused
each time she witnesses tyres burn
when he does a screeching u-turn.

Gear

Gary's normal routine of stress,
adrenaline rush to excess,
is effected by a bad cold.
However, refuses to fold,
won't succumb to fits of sneezing,
head dull-thumping and chest wheezing.
When colleagues feel slightly off-key
they will call in sick, stay away;
this man achieves more than his peers
even when stuck in second gear.

Richard Seal's *'Tides'*

Earth, gasping in drought,
is way beyond craving rain.
Concedes to fissures.

Staring at the wound,
gaping open, newly-dug,
awaits fade to grey.

Takes mum's hand and walks
beside her part of the way.
Journey has begun.

She cried for a cat
as a child; thanks to felines,
tears have never stopped.

Ben and Billy

Ben and Billy were best of friends,
but the beagles bickered as well;
they drove each other round the bend,
though rows were brief. Neither would dwell

too long on disputes over beds;
there were bigger concerns than that.
The biggest fear, it must be said
was how on Earth to foil the cat.

Nancy planned and plotted alone,
had more wit and guile than both dogs;
the feline confiscated bones,
Ben and Billy faced a hard slog

to come up with the slightest thing
which could stop the cat in her tracks;
always one step ahead, ran rings
round both, always avoiding flak.

The poor dogs always took the rap
over every breakage or mess;
often Nancy's work, not the chaps,
but the cat would never confess.

Richard Seal's *'Tides'*

In the end accepted defeat,
aware the feline ruled the roost;
scratched their noses, and stole meat treats.
The friends were in need of a boost.

The dogs then focused on the man
and woman who lived in their house;
could they succeed with Joe and Jan,
as they did not have feline nous?

Dogs looked for little victories
in a desperate quest to succeed;
started badly, Jan broke her knee
when she tripped over Billy's lead.

With country walks now out of reach
the pair played upstairs in the bath;
they broke the toilet, spilled some bleach,
incurring great upset and wrath.

The final straw occurred next day:
they damaged the rabbit hutches,
lawn and flower beds during play,
then Ben knocked Jan off her crutches.

Stuck in the doghouse once again,
the beleaguered pair had a hunch
they might have overtaxed their brains,
so lay down and waited for lunch.

Double Event

After her long relationship
had ended it felt like a trip
which had gone for years just stopped.
Although the girl's self-esteem dropped
and life seemed to turn upside down,
her fortune started turning round
the following day; opened up
to a workmate over a cup
of tea which extended to lunch.
Tears turned to laughter with a hunch
John's arrival just as Phil went
could be the best double event.

Untamed

Watching cat move through undergrowth
what strikes the watching girl the most
is that tabby fur against fronds
and the way long grasses respond
to the animal's intrusion
involves a kind of collusion,
unconscious, implicit, unnamed
between cat and nature, untamed.

Barbecue

There's nothing that Fred liked to do
more than having a barbecue;
the smell of charcoal, spitting fat
and clouds of smoke - loved all of that.

The cooking area was large,
Fred had to be the man in charge
hamburgers never tasted the same
when not barbecued in his name.

One day a health scare laid him low,
and the barbecue had to go.
Bought low fat food for his diet,
could not bring himself to try it.

Eventually he came to see
true benefits of broccoli;
the man had a new favourite dish:
boiled potatoes, spinach and fish.

Fred lost a lot of bulk and met
his target weight quickly, and yet
knew he could fall off the wagon,
a hot dogs binge could still happen.

Richard Seal's *'Tides'*

Shafts of light through trees
fall on couple lying, spent.
Cool air on flushing.

Teetering on brink,
gallows humour holds steady,
wisecracks stop the drop.

Friendship stands time's test,
pen pals for twenty five years.
They will never meet.

Beyond the back fence
woodlice are keen for a touch
of ball bent concave.

Richard Seal's *'Tides'*

Shower Curtain

Loved having a shower each day,
but one thing that got in her way
was the pesky plastic curtain.
Maxine always knew for certain
that it would wrap around wet skin.
In the end threw it in the bin,
got a walk-in shower installed.
Wondered, after a nasty fall,
if the curtain had still been there
would she have these ligament tears?

Colic

The infant shook off her colic
quickly in order to frolic;
on the floor, surrounded by toys,
she rolled making a noise
while laughing uncontrollably.

Her mother was relieved to see
a familiar look in Fran's eyes
of excitement, joy and surprise.
One happy squeeze of her finger
showed no discomfort had lingered.

Purse

When Pam thought she had lost her purse,
believed there could be nothing worse
than ringing banks to cancel cards -
She knew these things would be so hard.
Although the bag was found upstairs
this did not stop her doubts and cares;
always worried about the bills,
what would happen if she got ill?

Her husband took her in his arms,
spoke soothing words which tried to calm
but nothing seemed to work until
her feline became gravely ill.
When Monty hovered at death's door
the woman desired nothing more
than her cat's health. His survival
inspired Pam's joyful revival.

Best China

After half a century, Bill
holds Margery's hand tighter still;
a look tells more then words can say
as doctor shows them the x-ray.
Thinner each day, lattice of bones,
Bill's beloved wife never moans.
She still loves her afternoon tea,
the China set comes out at three.
Smiling, as she has always done,
the lady turns towards the sun.

Sound

Buster Keaton, The Great Stone Face,
highly acclaimed, secured a place
in silent movies' Hall of Fame;
the comedian made his name

acting, directing his own work.
Charlie Chaplin enjoyed the perks
of being silent clown number one,
his Tramp was a worldwide icon.

Harold Lloyd was different again:
bespectacled guy with a brain;
while comic chaos would descend
he got the sweet girl in the end.

Harry Langdon, pale babyface
darling of silents fell from grace
after 'Jazz Singer' caused regret
saying 'you ain't heard nothing yet.'

Laurel and Hardy stood alone,
with innocence and gentle tones;
unlike the others they survived
silent pictures' demise, both thrived

with the advent of sound movies.
Their voices perfect, fans agreed
the well loved pair richly deserved
to be not only seen but heard.

Rough

Shivers in coat, pulls collar tight
against another freezing night.
His old home is still standing there,
but man has struggled with despair
since his wife and kids moved away.
He had walked out on them one day,
exhausted by panic attacks,
and could never face going back.
At last the man has had enough
of life on the street, sleeping rough;
feels stronger, wants to try again,
take the first step out of the rain.

Survivor

Having struggled to find a way
to survive, Anna wants to stay
in England. While she understands
her degree is not in demand,
studies and works hard, never stops,
grateful for her job in a shop.
What sticks in this Polish girl's craw
is moaning, colleagues want much more.
When her Dad died working the land,
the whole family changed their plans;
without complaint, like her brothers
she sends money home to mother.

Richard Seal's *'Tides'*

Mum returns in cheese
melted over noodles; lives
in this pasta bowl.

This 'loveable rogue',
self-styled, was not liked until
the charade was dropped.

When he holds his wife
close decades dissolve to take
them back to first waltz.

Luxuriated
together in ripe peaches,
deep richness yielding.

Old Friends

Bridget cannot wait for her flight
to London to see some old pals
only has to wait three more nights
before boosting flagging morale.

She liked some girls more than others,
sadly best friend Kay won't be there;
hated Annie and her mother
while she could never take to Claire.

Sal and Sharon were very nice
for a while but they both turned cold;
once trusted, Ruth betrayed her twice.
Will they all return to the fold?

Suddenly seeing them again
is a prospect weighed down with dread;
Bridget decides she will abstain
and head off to Brighton instead.

Mum

Susan cannot help but wonder
what stress her birth Mum was under
when she gave her daughter away.
Conflicted, finds it hard to say
how she feels. No one is to blame,
but prefers not to know her name.
She reflects with a gentle sigh
and hint of a tear in her eye.

Vindaloo

Hurricane blast of Vindaloo
was an assault on the senses,
it shook his rafters as it blew
away all the man's defences.
Wiping tears away from his eyes,
sweat ran down the back of his shirt;
concluded it may not be wise
to tackle hot curries that hurt.
Yet the next time he came in
Mick could not face korma or dal;
going too mild seemed like a sin
so he braced himself for a Phall.

Cheekbones

Maxine defies sixty five years
with her high cheekbones and smooth skin;
Ensures that no grey hairs appear,
yet a brittleness lurks within.
She clutches puppies in her arms
when anxiousness intensifies,
with dogs she can come to no harm
is the hope in those troubled eyes.
Spends time in her friends' company
but she struggles after a while;
feels lost staring into her tea,
attempting to sustain a smile.

Sweets

Susie loved sweets as a child;
a chocolate mouse could drive her wild.
Turned away from games, eschewed sport,
preferring liquorice allsorts.

Most of all, the girl had a dream
to have unlimited ice cream;
assumed that she would be in bliss
if she spent all her cash on this.

Susie never lost the sweet tooth
that she had had throughout her youth,
but rationed the confectionery
and settled for saccharine in tea.

Then turning forty changed all that,
diet was knocked into a cocked hat.
For one day friends could not enter
without a box of soft centres.

Fifty seems a bigger milestone
so restraint will not be condoned;
no plans to travel, climb mountains,
just wants her own chocolate fountain.

Scan

Swallowing gingerly, Bill blows hard,
knows he cannot walk very far.
Beloved dog pulls on the lead
looking at her master to plead
for a chance to have a good run,
but Bill is well and truly done.
Has another coughing attack,
suspecting his cancer is back.
Plans to start a hospital ban,
he cannot face another scan.

Big Fish

Karen did not expect to receive
a special gift - could not believe
that her cat carried a fish,
much larger than a serving dish.
Put creature in water, then saw
that Montague had a wet paw.
She realised what had occurred
next door's pond must have been disturbed.
The cat could have stood watch for weeks,
then struck when on a winning streak.
Monty groomed himself, looking smug,
expecting a stroke or a hug.
Not impressed fruit of his labour
was taken back to the neighbours.
Never mind, he would bide his time
then return to scene of the crime.

Richard Seal's *'Tides'*

Ten years since she left
wound will not heal. Scab's brittle
knitting unstitches.

Doctor's prognosis
banishes pension worries:
focus on three months.

Shock as retina,
detaches itself, peels away
like old wallpaper.

Cheekbones to die for
are more pronounced through thin skin
in her final days.

Sofa

Frank never wanted to get off
the sofa - it felt warm and soft.
He would lie down watching TV
and relaxed while eating his tea.
But when his rescue cat appeared
she clearly had the same idea;
puss moved in on Frank's territory,
and before long the man could see
he was being shunted to one side.
There was no way to turn the tide,
While she stretched out, it seemed unfair
that Frank had to find a new chair.

Lazy

Bill thought everyone was crazy
when they said that he was lazy
Before any projects began,
he needed to take time to plan,
reflect, analyse and cogitate,
without worrying about dates.
Nothing got off the drawing board,
targets and deadlines were ignored;
When in the end they let him go,
little did the strategist know
most colleagues were barely aware
genius was no longer there.

Rhinestone Cat

On the circuit, in Rhinestone gear,
a country and western cat appears;
the Persian is a striking sight,
her white suit set against the night.

The usual topics aren't explored,
unrequited love is ignored;
she does not miss a Ginger Tom
who can play heart strings with aplomb.

She does not sing of loneliness
or broken lives left in a mess;
performing with her pink guitar,
Marcie is a true Nashville star.

For this cat, woe is not allowed,
her mission is to charm the crowd;
her songs tell how success is found
outwitting a series of hounds.

Replay

Holding his gaze through closed windows,
taking a few steps as train goes,
is a movie moment replayed
each time her boyfriend goes away.
Different clothes or a platform change,
some aspects may be re-arranged,
scene is sometimes framed in the rain
but feelings are always the same.

Chapter Four

Dead Leg

Meeting at the bus stop again
forty years on, remembers when
the best thing that a lad could learn
was how to give a Chinese burn.

His old pal Frank looks much the same.
He has gone bald, but not ashamed,
while Mike himself wears glasses now.
Feels sure his friend will still know how

to greet him on the proper way;
hoping that it will be okay,
steps forward, acting on his hunch
gives a dead leg and shoulder punch.

☐

Treasure Map

As a lad, had recurring dreams
about being on a pirate ship;
The legend Long John Silver seemed
to preside over thrilling trips.

In dreams Phil discovered a box
hidden below deck under ropes;
he managed to snap off the lock,
and the map inside gave him hope.

It showed a desert island where
a huge treasure chest could be found;
Phil knew he had to make it there
and find his fortune underground.

When the island came into view
Phil's adrenaline level soared;
unseen by any of the crew,
the lad disappeared overboard.

After swimming throughout the night,
his limbs felt as heavy as lead;
reaching the island at first light,
he felt lucky not to be dead.

Passing out on the stony beach,
Phil was shocked to wake up in bed;
the adventure now out of reach,
had dreams about nature instead.

Richard Seal's *'Tides'*

Sometimes found himself tantalised
by visions of silver and gold;
waking up cut him down to size
with the treasure trail turned stone cold.

As days turned into weeks Phil tried
to get back to the pirate plot.
Years later hopes have still not died,
for him, 'X' always marks the spot.

Revolving Doors

At the airport entrance Jo paused,
this was the place she first met Jim,
bemused at these revolving doors,
when she was propelled into him.

Laughter had been the cornerstone
of their friendship right from the start;
now they had spend six months alone,
over ten thousand miles apart.

His face online was not the same,
while she relished his smile and voice,
preferred him there to light her flame,
but from Sydney they had no choice.

Jim would be at arrivals now,
for Jo not a moment too soon;
at the revolving doors knew how
he would grapple her like a loon.

Zoe

Mr Perkins suffers slight flush,
aware of teenage student's crush.
Zoe slips the man extra prose,
scented with lavender or rose,
but he dents self esteem with lips
pursed over all her grammar slips;
appreciates words are heartfelt,
but such a shame they are mis-spelt.
She holds her breath, feels nervous when
he gives the girl six out of ten.

Class Clown

Lad embraced his role as class clown,
with jokes and high jinks up his sleeve;
most at home when fooling around
and the teacher got no reprieve.

Miss Smith felt browbeaten each day,
in the end she could take no more;
determined now to find a way
to fight back and even the score.

A few wisecracks at lad's expense
deflated his sails fairly soon;
still had a laugh, took no offence
at the popping of some balloons.

Richard Seal's *'Tides'*

Fleeting hope at pause
by cat closing in on prey
lasts but a second.

Turning one hundred,
instead of a telegram
wants a bungee jump.

Life experience
and passage of time can help
close an open mind.

Hearing thunder, tries
climbing a tall tree in time
to catch the lightning.

Tough

Looking at her daughter, Jenny
remembers well being her age;
teenage Bess does not have many
problems. When she was at that stage

lacked confidence, education;
riddled with anxiety, fear;
no money, tough situation,
waiting for baby to appear.

Bess gives Jenny a heavy glare.
Mum had it easy, never worked;
stayed at home, it does not seem fair
how she cruised, enjoying life's perks.

Norah keeps her own counsel and smiles;
daughter and granddaughter are plucky,
stubborn, passionate, have some style.
Both are incredibly lucky.

Fanning

Señora teeters on the brink
of despair, her English class stinks!
Confused about conjugation,
perplexed by pronunciation,
grammar, tenses keep going wrong,
she dare not attempt a diphthong.
Teacher is far too pedantic,
Marta's self-fanning is frantic.

Tigress

Customers have been known to quake
in fear as Alexandra waits
on tables during busy hours.
The waitress seems to have the power
to turn impatient folk to stone
before they have the chance to moan.
Spares no-one, has become renowned
for shooting the toughest types down.
Her grey eyes harden and lips set
to snarl in an unveiled threat
at a request for Earl Grey Tea.
Those who asked are tempted to flee.

However, on another day,
Alex can keep demons at bay.
It appears the girl can decide
to become charm personified.
The tigress then turns pussy cat
with her friendly banter off pat.
Nothing is now too much trouble,
she fetches drinks at the double.
While free biscuits are handed out,
no-one should be in any doubt
the girl reserves the right to turn
and complacent folk can get burned.

Monologue

Sally loves her friend, and yet
there is no subtle way to get
her off the phone when in full flow;
Teresa does not seem to know
how to listen or to allow
Sal to get a word in somehow.
She tried in vain to find a gap
for years, but has had to adapt;
the only way she can stay sane
is to do something else, refrain
from engaging until aware
of a voice saying 'Are you there?'
Speaks quickly, she has got the knack,
before the monologue comes back.

Lycra-Clad

Malcolm cycles to work each day,
he finds it the easiest way
to exercise, though colleagues tease
him mercilessly, such a wheeze
as it brings a smile to their lips
when he flashes bicycle clips,
lime green or a bright shade of red.
While taking ribbing in good stead
about his gaudy Lycra clothes,
chapped cheeks and semi-frozen nose,
he wonders if they laugh so hard
when crawling along in their cars.

Cape

As a boy, loved gothic escape,
he would wear a black cape;
more than ready to misbehave,
he always returned from the grave.
Lurking under big sister's bed
he jumped out and relished her dread.
Laughter stopped when Meg died, aged ten,
Jamie never dressed up again.
Yet he still smiles, when on a whim,
she has her own fun haunting him.

Late in Life

Bachelor George wed late in life;
did not expect to find a wife.
June was vivacious and so sweet
she swept the shy man off his feet;
married within months, in a whirl,
they were blessed with two gorgeous girls.

After thirty wonderful years
June's breast cancer returned as feared.
When she lost the battle at last,
George was distraught, went downhill fast
for a while, avoided the phone,
and spent his days drinking alone.

But then a new chapter began
when dear daughters helped him make plans.
Once accepting his survival,
he slowly embraced revival;
starting going out, feeling calm,
beloved June still on his arm.

Richard Seal's *'Tides'*

Jumping from a plane
parachutist is tempted
not to pull the chord.

The hurt that he caused
in several relationships
is doubling back.

Woman lost herself
chatting hands-free in the car;
tree ended the call.

If she concentrates
can levitate, float above
life with arms outstretched.

Chariots

Dreamed of images, strange ideas;
they filled his head from ear to ear;
and yet when writing all these down
the process always made him frown.

Winged chariots he saw at night
by break of day had taken flight,
the crazy stream of consciousness
had dwindled into something less.

The creatures with five legs, two heads
on waking became dogs instead,
while the beautiful three-eyed Queen
turned into a woman in jeans.

Cities ruled by genies and ghouls
by morning were towns full of fools;
the head-height drifts of purple snow
melted away as the cock crowed.

Concluded that the way to keep
the magic was to stay asleep,
but he could not do this all day
so had to find another way.

In the end he came to accept
that it was not fair to expect
mere words to do more than respond
to the powers which lay way beyond.

Sick Note

Hated sport growing up, no fun
to be found in having to run.
No time for cricket, could not see
the point of hockey or rugby.
Last man picked for the football team,
this did not affect self esteem
because his focus was elsewhere
and the student could daydream there.
Solution was found in the end:
stood on the side-lines watching friends;
Nice and warm in thick overcoat,
in possession of a sick note.

First Date

Watching his dear wife take a sip
of tea, Charlie lets his mind slip
back forty years to their first date,
and his nervous, excited state.
Still thrills at that coy smile, delights
at her pale blue eyes which invite
him to move in closer; that voice
so alluring, makes him rejoice
in having chills sent down his spine.
The man feels grateful all the time,
has been known to shiver and shake
over a slice of Joanne's cake.

Bath Mat

It seemed as if Grandma's bath mat
had always housed her aged cat.
The old rug was a fixture there,
getting increasingly threadbare.

It must have felt so many toes,
and countless dirty feet - who knows
how many verrucas were found,
and did corns and bunions abound?

Then again, the feline stands guard;
accessing her bed would be hard.
It might have been used just by her
and coated with black and white fur.

Marathon

Runner feels relief and delight
at the long-awaited sight
of the marathon's finish line.
Hope to have beaten his best time;
at the end he can barely jog
after such an exhausting slog
So many times Max hit the wall,
but dug deep and refused to stall
or allow leaden limbs to stop.
Final race won, now fit to drop.

Richard Seal's *'Tides'*

Relentless rainfall
holds sway. One lapse and sunshine
sneaks out between clouds.

Sitting on the fence
he cannot help wavering
in prevailing wind.

Summer days offer
a selection of fine cones
filled with seething wasps.

Atop a haystack
couple take risk of finding
a needle within.

'Happy Meal'

Struggles into tight plastic seat
amid screaming kids; starts to eat
a supersized burger and fries,
with chicken nuggets on the side.
Feels bloated within a few bites,
and his mood darkens at the sight
of the sugar-laden milkshake.
Wonders if he made a mistake
by not choosing a 'Happy Meal'
it might have 'less is more' appeal.

Fight

Not having seen Jean for a while,
Barbara breaks the ice with a smile,
chit chat about this and that -
their ailments, grandchildren, and cats.
Holding forth over cups of tea,
each assumes her friend will agree
with opinions not start a debate
on how best to make Britain great.
One's Lefty views, other's far right
makes for an uncomfortable fight
played out through flushed cheeks
and clipped tones
as anger would not be condoned.
Looking down at a custard slice,
it no longer looks very nice.

Dawned

Slumped on the sofa, Mick scratches;
bored of watching football matches,
he flicks between TV stations.
Considers his situation
for a moment, but the man lacks
self awareness; lazy and slack,
he can't be bothered to reflect
on feckless lack of self-respect.
Assumes, with inner light dismissed,
that he has always felt like this.

Predator

Owl shifts slightly, moves position,
focused on his nightly mission
to catch himself a mouse a rat;
but so often foiled by the cat
who breezes in and selfishly
usurps the bird's territory.
The time has come to have his say
and scare the tabby fool away.
Puss glances at the hawk-like beak
and sharp talons. If she could speak
feline would surely tell the owl
where he could put his fearsome scowl.

Standards

Throughout her long life, Gran believed
that Labour fell short, felt aggrieved
and said the so-called Socialists
in centre ground should be dismissed.
However, she hated Tories,
and told many horror stories
concerning right-wing nastiness.
She said that no one should have less,
and equality would occur
when standards of life rose to hers.

Tonic

The woman had come to relish
her daily pick-me-up, cherished
the special effervescent mix
of caffeine and codeine. Her fix
would see life's sharp edges removed,
stress was reduced, nerves were soothed.
However, in time something changed;
the stuff seems weaker, it is strange
that head-pounding has got stronger
and seems to last a lot longer.
Now all the pain relief has gone
concludes her tonic is a con.

Bat

At the fringes of the campsite
in Seville, bats come out at night.
They hang on boughs, lying in wait
to catch insects many folk hate.
Mosquitos and flies are consumed,
but humans lazily assume
these mammals are malevolent,
connected with vampires, hell-bent
on associating with death.
Although tourists could not care less
about bats while having a beer,
they ought to hold these creatures dear.

Toyshop

Looking around toy superstores
for Granny is a rare reward
and a lifelong secret pleasure.
Tells grandson to find a treasure,

choose anything that he desires.
But the boy loses interest, tires
and wants to play games on his phone.
Excitement is Granny's alone

as she squeezes creatures that squeak,
things that tinkle, dollies that speak.
As a child, play brought joy and hope;
she still has her first skipping rope.

Richard Seal's *'Tides'*

Boy stares up at cloud
blackening into nightfall.
Stars are unwelcome.

Wind took the man's breath,
absorbed him into its power
to kick back, destroy.

Ruined house in Spain
held together just barely
by shadows and dreams.

Break of day picks up
interweaved threads of sunlight
abandoned last night.

Ears

Katie could never get enough
of spending time with her cat, Fluff.
She was driven to joyful tears
by the sight of her Tabby's ears.
From the start they were extra large,
so dominant, clearly in charge
of her cat's physical presence.
As the years went by it made sense
his body would grow and catch up
but it was never quite enough
to topple the big ears from power.

This feline would never cower;
battled illness bravely throughout
his long life, it was not in doubt
that Katie would need a long time
to mourn her dear partner in crime.
When little sister Dew arrived
the family were not surprised
that this new black cat in the house
had tiny ears just like a mouse.

Retreat

On the retreat the silence seemed
like an all-encompassing dream;
a profound sense of inner peace
found a calm place beyond release
where thinking became illusion.
Without day to day intrusions,
meditation helped her to see
that she only needed to be.

Achilles Heel

Mr Jeeves, the black and white cat
can take or leave you, that is that;
after lunch he wrinkles his nose
before heading off for a doze.
For a little while kept concealed
one and only Achilles Heel;
If you give the cat's ears a tweak
his reaction is quite unique.
Jeeves sends ripples through his fur
as he starts to dribble and purr;
both eyes roll around in his head
whilst he kneads and pulls at his bed.
However, the display is brief
as he curtails this light relief;
with composure at last regained,
expression returns to disdain.

Chapter Five

Skipping

Flushed by first love, dazed and confused,
Sam cannot help being amused
and not in the least bit alarmed
by a desire to flap her arms
while skipping around her bedroom.
Hoping her joy will not end soon,
feels compelled to sit down and write
about her emotions all night.
By dawn euphoria has been shared,
copied, pasted, sent everywhere.

□

Sick

Man has a hunch his lack of sleep,
upset stomach, headache which keeps
pace with a sore throat, might be due
to a nasty dose of the flu.
But what if it is serious,
a condition mysterious
that can defy medical science?
Christopher's over-reliance
on a range of medication
will not help the situation.
After feeling dehydrated,
he switches to constipated
before a trapped wind/heart attack/
stroke fells the hypochondriac.

Password Protected

Has problems with passwords, forgets
where she wrote them down, has not yet
worked out a way for bits of paper
she needs not to get lost later.
None of her details can be spied
with accounts locked, access denied.
Her computer is so secure
now she can't get in any more.

Water

As a child she was made to place
a glass of water by her bed
every night. She would pull a face
because of the thought in her head

there would be a fly floating dead
on the surface the next morning;
the prospect filled the girl with dread,
she cried at times without warning.

Teenage years have dispelled those fears,
now drinks bottled water always;
although new worries have appeared,
such as keeping hunger at bay.

Water staves off her appetite
to some extent, and helps her skin;
but thinks about food late at night,
and things she gave up to get thin.

Not You

Nicholas felt hurt and confused
and more than a little bit bruised
when Jo told him he was so good
and really hoped he understood
that she prefers to date bad boys;
loves excitement, danger and noise.
Dwelling on 'It's me, it's not you'
he can see that this might be true.

Leprechaun

During her childhood in Sligo
only child Sinead came to know
she would have a passion always
for Leprechauns and all their ways.

She had read about them in books,
convinced they were real, tried to look
out for Leprechauns now and then;
knew she would find one, not sure when.

It started one day in a field,
seeking a pot of gold concealed;
however, at the rainbow's end
appeared a magical green friend.

The little man with the large beard
did not seem in the least weird.
He was wearing a coat and hat,
and was well-fed rather than fat.

He said he made and mended shoes
by day but could never refuse
any chance to have light relief
by indulging in some mischief.

When introduced to Sinead's cat
they became firm friends - that was that.
The two would head out late at night
run riot through gardens until light.

Richard Seal's *'Tides'*

The pair would trample over flowers,
chase barn owls in the early hours,
pop in and out of cat-flaps too,
raided fridges and no one knew

until next morning when the cheese
and meat was found to have been seized;
householders were concerned to find
boot prints and whiskers left behind.

When Sinead moved to the U.K.
her cat came, but Leprechaun stayed.
At first the girl cried floods of tears,
but then her green friend re-appeared.

Still prowled at night with her feline,
took to taking cream cakes and wine;
both enjoyed lemon meringue pie,
and looked for new sweet treats to try.

Sinead's cat is now twenty one,
and her Leprechaun has not gone;
he keeps a low profile at home,
an undercover garden gnome.

No one knows that her friend is there,
during daylight he takes great care,
only Sinead can see him blink
and her cat gets a cheeky wink.

Richard Seal's *'Tides'*

Spider has its home
atop old Wellington boots.
Web adult size nine.

Walking out in Spring,
finds new growth in garden:
freshly built ant hills.

Moles take out their maps,
make their own plans for the stripes
mowed into the lawn.

The courting couple
monopolising the bench
grapple with splinters.

Uniform

On principle, the Englishman
living in Spain imposed a ban
on himself from ever wearing
the tourist uniform, bearing
his flesh in tee-shirts and shorts.
He had vowed never to be caught
in these clothes. Wants to emulate
the dress code of his Spanish mates,
but in jacket and trousers sweats,
the inside of his shirt gets wet.
Struggling badly in the heat,
refuses to admit defeat;
the Brit collapses in the town,
ends up in a hospital gown.

Cards

He made a point of counting cards,
calculating odds. It was hard,
knew his credit would be refused;
convinced himself he could not lose
time after time, and yet he did.
Always outmanoeuvred, outbid
and outwitted in intense games.
Although the outcome was the same,
he kept coming back for more.
Savings diminished, knew the score.
One final time he bet the lot,
and, riding his luck, scooped the pot.

White Lie

Peter told a lot of white lies:
assured his mum he loved her pies
and that he studied hard at school,
where he would never play the fool.

Growing up, he used to tell Mum
that he was going out with chums,
but would come back for tea in time.
He seldom returned before nine.

Later with his own family
the white lies were still plain to see:
he was not inclined to confess
when he hated his daughter's dress.

Peter told his kids not to fear,
the Disney trip might come next year;
he managed to convince himself
not to worry about his health.

On finding himself short of breath,
denied that he was scared to death;
collapsing when out with his son,
he claimed to have had too much fun.

When doctors showed her Peter's scan
partner Lisa said to the man
that everything would be okay,
she knew that was the only way.

Obscured

The man grins wryly at the thrill
he felt that afternoon, feels still,
about his and Jane's first photo.
How could he and his girlfriend know
that when they got the pictures back,
those of his friends and brother Jack
would be fine, but both would be stunned
that they were obscured by a thumb.
Robert suspected that their waitress,
who had spilled coffee on Jane's dress,
did it on purpose with a grin
perhaps because she fancied him.

Ready Meal

Couple tucked in to home-made fare,
prepared with the greatest of care.
Took it in turns with each other
to cook dinner just like mother.
Relished sensual pleasure shared.
Now alone, Edward is aware
life has gone downhill since Gill died.
Looks at his shop-bought cottage pie,
and knows that he will never feel
able to face a ready meal.

Richard Seal's *'Tides'*

Dog's medication
finally liberates fur.
Ticks retreat for now.

An awkward silence
is all friends reunited
can share ten years on.

Expensive cat frame,
assembled by her humans,
sure to be ignored.

Man's dark humour twists
with a grin maniacal,
throaty cackle, cracked.

Neighbour

Young woman on a long-haul flight
cannot sleep at all, spends the night
imagining what existence might

be like for the man next to her -
What joy and sadness has occurred?
Is his view black or white or blurred
into shadows and shades of grey?

He may have suffered pain and strife,
the loss of his beloved wife.
Will he open up about life
when the darkness at last makes way?

Heroes

Samantha finds life-blood in books.
As a child loved libraries, would look
in awe through the adult section,
novels awaiting inspection.
Inspired by covers which were bent
and dog-eared corners; journeys meant
to be explored time and again,
where imagination reigns.
As pages pass through her fingers,
joyful expectations linger.
Characters materialise,
villains thrive, heroes never die.

Fifty Years

Married for fifty years, Bill takes Jane's hand
then they raise a toast to this special night;
no words are required as both understand
that everything is going to be alright.

The kids have long since grown up and moved out,
but they all love to return to the fold;
relive happy childhood, no fear or doubt,
in a place where no one really gets old.

The end is approaching, both are ailing
but the couple are simply not prepared
to dwell on anything but plain sailing,
and luxuriating in being there.

Despite their five decades of history
Jane has retained an air of mystery.

Extreme Old Age

Having reached his extreme old age
Patrick finds himself at the stage
of wondering how he got here.
The prospect of death holds no fear,
feels peaceful contentment instead
about approaching one hundred.
No longer wastes time on worry,
knows there is no need to hurry
Slightly amused that each day seems
like a fresh and vibrant daydream.

Sold

Natalie would sell anything.
It started with old clothes and rings,
but before long excitement gripped
and her sense of perspective slipped.

As things spiralled out of control,
these are some things Nat wanted sold:
A bag of keys with unknown locks,
fifteen multi-coloured odd socks,
two books with the last page missing,
photos of two strangers kissing,
boxes of wine glasses with cracks,
three guitars with the strings gone slack,
suede jacket with elbow patches,
LPs with assorted scratches,
a range of tins without labels
and a woodworm-ridden table.

It was high time that she was stopped
but what approach should friends adopt?
This was someone who thought it fine
to auction off her Gran online.

Aunt Shirl

The kids all loved Dad's sister Shirl
with her striped skirts and strings of pearls.
Their Aunt was so fond of joking,
enjoyed light-hearted fun-poking.
In her forties Shirl ran a pub,
and had a great time, but the rub
was drinking too much with her friends.
It all got too much in the end.

The woman slowed down by the stage
of reaching her late middle age;
the colour deepened, slightly bruised,
but she still twinkled and amused.
Accepted health problems with grace,
trademark smile never left her face;
after death the lady revived,
her legend continues to thrive.

Beach Shirt

To some extent Mike can avert
dark feelings when in a beach shirt.
More upbeat in flamingo pink,
colleagues do not know what to think
when the man parades pineapples
proudly across his chest. Grappling
with sinking blackness, feels secure
in palm trees on cotton, azure.

Richard Seal's *'Tides'*

The busker forgets
that he cannot make ends meet,
during the chorus.

Always so polite
to justify fingers flicked
behind the veneer.

In the dead of night
fox strolls alone on the lawn;
dapper by moonlight.

Woman smiles, knowing
she looks stunning, likes to strike
men dumb at first sight.

Ducks

They used to feed bread to the ducks
but often hit upon bad luck:
Huge swans appeared to muscle in
a battle they would always win.

The woman and her favourite niece
both tried to throw a little piece
directly to a duck or two
but all the swans already knew

this ploy and always got there first.
Eventually the pair felt cursed,
and gave up, but they might just try
once more with cake and cottage pie.

Version

When she found the suicide note
inside a pocket of his coat,
something was amiss, Cass could tell
she did not come out of it well.
However, it did not take long
to put right what he had done wrong.
The version that the woman wrote
was full of glowing anecdotes
and self-loathing. It was inspired,
while Bernard's one went on the fire.

Board

Blackboard, covered with dust traces,
has not seen any young faces,
whether keen, mischievous or bored,
for years since being put in store.
Traditional desks stand nearby;
these abandoned things wonder why
they fell out of favour one day,
and were left to rot, locked away.
Each hopes days of chalk and ink pens
for old times' sake return again.

The Hole

What does it mean to see a man
walking through a cornfield alone?
We cannot truly understand
if a dog takes against his bone.
What lurks beneath the the stagnant stuff
that we see on top of a ditch?
The rabbit knows he knows enough
without questioning every twitch;
lives in the moment in a place
where thinking does not take its toll.
Fleeing from a predator's face,
he disappears into his hole.

Missing

Young Tommy Perkins was last seen
in the village three days ago.
For his family it has been
a dreadful nightmare. If you know
anything, have information
which you think might shed some light
on this urgent situation
contact the police, day or night.
This article has been revealed,
having spent twelve years in the loft;
paper protected and concealed
fragile ornaments in a box.
Fading newsprint crumbles away
in the woman's helpless fingers;
Internet has nothing to say
about the case. Sadness lingers.

Marble

Feels like a stone, having been kicked,
ricocheting off a curb, flicked
up through an arc, then a sharp drop
into long damp grass where she stops.
Or, like a small marble, chinking,
she hops on thin bars of the drain
then falls into dark mud, stinking,
never to resurface again.

Richard Seal's *'Tides'*

Suitors selected,
favoured awhile, drawn in by
eyelashes batted.

After their breakup,
man's pieces, reassembled,
now no longer fit.

Class rebel revels
in her secret cell before
shock confiscation.

Hikers, spent in heat,
regarded with indifference
by cool, one-eyed cat.

Richard Seal's *'Tides'*

Swamp

The friends loved going out to play,
ignored warnings to stay away
from areas of marshy ground
where untold dangers could be found.
Sandra cannot forget the sight
of Elizabeth's desperate plight
in the swamp on the edge of town
mercilessly sucking her down.
Sandra tried to grasp slimy arms
to haul the youngster out of harm,
but it was futile; knows those eyes
will sear her soul until she dies.
The swamp may have long since been drained
but those screams of terror remain.

Abandoned Car

Thick grass, long undisturbed, slaps limbs
from all sides with wet blades that cling.
The gate has terminal disease,
wood crumbling like Caerphilly cheese.
The farm appears long derelict,
there was no way Chris could predict
he would find an abandoned car.
Unlikely to get very far,
there would be no quick getaway
in shell full of rust and decay;
however, rat in drivers seat
has not yet accepted defeat.

Nuzzled

Black cat nuzzling her human leaves
the man feeling good, he believes
that the fact he is not ignored,
receives head rubs and flexing paws
means that Jezebel holds him dear.
For the feline one thing is clear:
she must manipulate her pet
to ensure all her needs are met.
If his standards start going down
she won't hesitate to leave town.
But things have not quite gone to plan,
Jez has grown quite fond of the man.

Healing Hands

So many people told the man
that he was blessed with healing hands;
warmth emanated from his palms
and soothed any sense of alarm.
On shoulders as solid as rock
his fingertips somehow unblocked
deep-rooted tension to release
a new-found sense of inner peace.
Although the man has passed away
his magic remains to this day.
When distressing problems occur
Ben's wife still feels his hand in hers.

Chapter Six

Scattered

The girl had always been able
to sit at the kitchen table,
with her family every day
though her eyes were far far away.
Jane had a particular stare
when she was residing elsewhere.
As an adult she does it still:
goes to a private place at will.
Finds peace when life is in tatters;
takes her own ashes to scatter.

☐

Das Chippy

German adventurer Stefan
is a happy-go-lucky man;
so well-travelled, loves the U.K.
and looks for any chance to say
something to locals drinking ale;
He asks one if his crisps are stale.
On a mission to try some fish
and chips, the famous English dish;
he reacts with unbridled glee
to limp cod and takeaway tea.
For him the only thing lacking
is the real newspaper wrapping.
So joyful when it starts to rain,
this is the last link in the chain.

Blackbird

When Frank got home, he did not expect
to see a blackbird standing erect
on a tall shelf in the living room;
seemed unlikely to be leaving soon.
Not sure what to do to help the bird,
but then something surprising occurred:
it jumped down and casually walked out,
hopped through the cat-flap, no sign of doubt.
Two hours later feline Bruce returned;
the mystery was unsolved, nothing learned.
After dinner, the cat shook his head,
but black feathers turned up in his bed.

Right

Annabel has always refused
to talk politics, gets accused
by friends of being too right wing;
they pick up on the slightest thing.
She hesitates to share her views,
the arguments leave her confused.
All she really wants is the best
for friends and family, not less
than their years of hard work deserve;
talk of welfare gets on her nerves.
If feels as if she stands alone
trying to look out for her own.
Left or right? It seems far too tense
to be on one side of the fence.

Buddies

The two friends had met on the train,
clicked straightaway, laughed like a drain;
Vicky's razor-sharp acid wit
left Jane fearing her sides would split.
While they were best buddies for years,
darkness deepened; Vic disappeared
without trace one winter's morning.
She said nothing, left no warning.
Jane likes to recall that first day
when nothing could stand in the way
of impressions of the train guard
and giggling impossibly hard.

Richard Seal's *'Tides'*

Virus, believed gone,
mutates and regenerates
for renewed assault.

Shadow on the bench
is a man shrunk in sunshine,
blank in lifetime lost.

Regrets linger, long
to repent. Duties to serve
until the last breath.

Man feels nearly fit
for a hearse, saved from the brink
by a nurse's wink.

Den

As a child, every now and then
Jim would hide away in his den.
Deep in the wood, high in the trees
the youngster could do what he pleased.

In the den one day Jim was caught
by surprise while wrapped up in thought;
a grey squirrel entered his room,
bushy tale bristling in the gloom.

The creature fixed him with a glare
and asked what he was doing there.
Slack-jawed with shock, the lad stuttered,
squirrel said 'Speak up, don't mutter!"

She was clearly annoyed to see
this interloper in her tree.
Remarked 'There are things to be found
for humans to do on the ground!'

Jim recovered his senses, smiled,
spoke to the squirrel for a while.
He learned she just wanted a home,
a warm, safe place to call her own.

The youngster's heart went out to her,
but then a great idea occurred
to him, and the new friends agreed
a timeshare they hoped would succeed.

Richard Seal's *'Tides'*

Early mornings and late at night
the den was the squirrel's by rights;
Hers to use when the light was dim,
at other times the place was Jim's.

Squirrel loved living in the hut,
reserved one corner for her nuts.
When the boy's friends came to the den
he stressed this pile was not for them.

In time the squirrel used it more
than the youngster and she implored
Jim for more time for gatherings
where furry pals could dance and sing.

The lad lost interest in the end
and saw woodland creatures descend
to take over his childhood pad.
He was actually rather glad.

Decades later the man went back
to the location of his shack.
Despite not seeing it for years,
his old den had not disappeared.

To his joy he spotted a cat,
two squirrels, a stoat and a bat.
Reassured that they loved their house,
when he got a wave from a mouse.

Slingshot

Returning to old school playground
twenty years on, memories abound;
those pea-shooters and catapults
return to the smiling adult.
With practice, his aim had improved:
poor Gill's Alice band was removed;
this achievement improved morale
and prompted high-fives with his pals.
Now a teacher, the man is armed
with empty threats, and feels alarmed;
standing in class he is fair game
for verbal slingshots to take aim.

Chance

Man stops in his tracks at the sight
of his first crush one balmy night
alone on the bus thirty years on.
At school she was the only one
for him; felt excited and scared
when he was invited to share
her Tizer using just one straw.
The lad knew he could not afford
to let such a chance pass him by.
However, then as now, too shy;
instead of a smile and 'hello'
he watches her get up and go.

Richard Seal's *'Tides'*

Purses lips, partner
needs to be knocked into shape
or kicked into touch.

At the carousel
baggage-handler burst through flaps
riding a suitcase.

Friends made at school gate
on the first day may take years
for you to shake off.

Fond of phone boxes;
thrilled to snatch snippets before
being caught by pips.

Exam

Joy does not mind taking exams,
she is an adrenaline fan.
When under pressure does her best,
this woman is not phased by tests.
However, she cannot rejoice
when questions are multiple choice.
Hates to select A, B or C
as she often favours all three
or none of the options at all.
At such times she goes to his wall,
and the way to set herself free
is to answer them all with 'D'.

First Job

Approaching retirement, Don thinks
back over time passed in a blink.
His favourite job without a doubt
was the first one - he would go out
With colleagues for a pint or two,
had boozy fun at the work's do.
He got involved in an affair
with a married manager there.
When Suzanne's husband disappeared
the secret lovers lived in fear
for a while that he would be found.
However, when the dust died down
Don moved in, and four decades on
the man's memory has almost gone.

Gentle Man

All his family agree that Ken
is the gentlest of men;
the man has devoted his life
to caring for his sons and wife.
He seems to spend most of the day
looking out for nice things to say.

Little do they know that this chap
keeps a dark secret under wraps;
at the time people thought it weird
when the widow Joan disappeared.
Ken felt stifled by mum's control,
while spite and moaning took its toll.

One day an accident occurred:
she fell downstairs; although Ken heard
the crash and cries, he made a choice
to take no notice of her voice.
Later the man was mortified
to find that his mother had died.

With blind panic gripping him tight
he took her body out that night
and buried it deep in the woods.
Resolved from then on to do good;
Twenty years on, no-one can find
a character so warm and kind.

And yet, from time to time he finds
mother returning to his mind.
Ken beseeches her to forgive,
to rest in peace and let him live.
She says nothing about the crime,
he knows she is biding her time.

Pylon

As a child, seemed the only one
to have an interest in pylons.
There used to be some in the fields
behind the garden; he would feel
intrigued by the low humming sound
that they made when he was around.
The things looked like great climbing frames,
would they make him burst into flames
as his anxious parents had warned?
It was a theory that he scorned.
But they moved before he could try
to ascend the tower and not die.
The lad felt it was so unfair
the reason was a cancer scare!

Applause

Loves to milk a round of applause,
every time he gets an award
for services to comedy,
or charity work with no fee.
With superstardom now in reach,
he makes a long and boring speech;
gives credit for his fame and wealth
to nobody else but himself.
Morning brings an end to the scene
when he leaves this recurring dream.

Richard Seal's *'Tides'*

The two old rivals
Oloroso-fortified
now reach an accord.

Body turned, bedsheets
churned; tumble into slumber
as alarm clock shocks.

Man was so sedate,
laid back, chilled out; took a while
to tell when he died.

Microwaved pasta
takes him back to mum's apron
and home-cooked childhood.

Death by Chocolate

Impatient with breaded mushrooms,
Caroline eyes a dessert spoon;
Indifferent about her roast pork,
she fiddles with a gateau fork.
Has no desire to take a break,
as both of her hands start to shake.
The third course must never be cut:
she chooses death by chocolate.

Last Time

The first time Linda let it go,
attempted to go with the flow;
the next time it felt like a strain,
but this turned into searing pain.
Awoke in a hospital bed,
convinced she was already dead;
then in an instant, levels dropped
her line went flat and bleeping stopped.
In final moments light and calm
dispelled residual alarm.

Twenty Five

Looking at his wife's sleeping face
Mark knows that nothing could replace
this sight at the start of each day.
He struggles to find words to say
to Jackie which truly express
the depth of his feelings; so blessed
at her side for twenty five years.
Smiles to himself and sheds a tear
on silver anniversary
as he heads downstairs to make tea.

Lampshade

Bill would put a pink lampshade on his head,
wear curtains, anything daft he could find;
stick pens up his nose, or pencils instead,
if he could get a laugh he did not mind.

Diane also had a comic routine
which involved terrible karaoke;
she was the most eccentric Dancing Queen,
and Bill's hysterics was a joy to see.

Together they would perform for their friends,
improvising; a natural double act.
The three kids were driven around the bend,
all of them convinced their parents were cracked.

In old age Bill and Diane stayed the same,
indulged in high jinks with their walking frames.

Jonesey

When a volunteer was required
one man raised his hand with desire
to be the first to climb the rope,
even though his arms could not cope.

A butcher by day, but at night
had no ration books in his sights.
This was no time to think of meat
when facing invasion, defeat.

The oldest man in the platoon,
Jones had no plans to give up soon;
had seen and done it all before,
and was always ready for war.

Never off duty, worked so hard,
this stalwart of the town's Home Guard
was indefatigable, strong;
knew action would come before long.

He geed his colleagues up of course,
determined to be a life force.
On the man's eightieth birthday,
If he could do it, so could they.

The Captain knew that if required
Jones would step up first to be fired
out of a cannon into woods
then do it again if he could.

Gags

The first joke that he ever told
was not his - it was rather old.
The second one was much the same,
but he refused to take the blame
for the reaction it received.
It seemed the man truly believed
he could do a show with encores
with gags that had been done before.
This approach did not serve him well,
but writing his own jokes was hell.
The comedian had worse in store,
they hated his stuff even more.

Wig

For many years Vince was appalled
at the prospect of going bald.
When his hair began to fall out
he was tempted to scream and shout.
To stave off baldness for a while
he attempted a range of styles.
The desperate man reached a nadir
with combovers borne out of fear.
Then one day he had had enough
Vince now likes to send himself up.
He has brightly coloured toupees
and wears a different one each day.

Richard Seal's *'Tides'*

In pavement battle
pram and shopping trolley trumped
by a man's guide dog.

Smiles at reflection;
taps the glass, takes a step back,
and winks at herself.

Travel plans are packed
and ready, but dreams delayed
awhile by night shifts.

She raises a toast
to her husband at sunset.
Twinkles at twilight.

Post Box

For decades it has stood with pride
with important contents inside;
This feature of the village green,
beside the phone box, could be seen
ready and waiting come what may
for whatever mail came its way.
Years ago they removed the phone,
it was not used so no one moaned.
Time's passing has taken a toll,
but the post box achieved its goal:
refuses to dwell on the past,
will do its duty to the last.
paint is peeling, letters are rare
but they are still treated with care.

Patient

Kenneth has problems with his knees,
he struggles with COPD,
and suffers with pain which lingers
in his arthritic fingers.
Yet the man always stays upbeat,
brushes off angina, flat feet,
makes the patients laugh while they wait
for doctor to spell out their fate.
Ken takes the bad news in his stride,
has a slim chance, but never mind;
while survival prospects are grim,
why can't the one in ten be him?

Jose

It happened many years ago,
Pat is the only one who knows
what became of Alistair White
who vanished without trace that night.
Every time he travels by plane
recalls Jose Luiz's name;
does the man have that passport still,
and is he living in Brazil?

Impression

Her impressions were uncanny.
As a child perfected Nanny
with her distinctive laughing snort
and unfortunate facial wart.
The youngster liked to do a turn,
aping her music teacher's gurns.
Siblings did not get off lightly,
featuring in girl's fun nightly:
Brother cringed hearing nasal tones,
sister winced at whining and moans.
But within Rose a sadness stirred:
why did no one try to do her?

Meg

Jack Russell, when she was rescued,
was so desperate for love and food.
Her eyes showed life had been rotten,
a wretched time best forgotten.
New owners have let Meg become
cherished as the favourite one.
Always installed at mother's side,
sleeps on her rug but woe betide
anyone daring to come close
to the one she covets the most.
As her guardian, the dog lets rip
with a low warning growl and nip.

Dream Cats

Fliss had a lovely purple cat
who lived in her room on a mat;
A yellow one purred on demand
whenever she saw the girl's hand.

The third feline, this one bright red,
slept beside Felicity's head
with one paw resting on her face,
which felt like the most natural place.

On waking up, found her real boy
having fun with his cat nip toy;
loved the creatures she dreamt about
but Max she could not do without.

Inspired

Loves rolling and controlling words,
sweet rhythms and rhymes can be heard
resonating in the man's mind.
Whenever he wants to rewind,
writes poems for relaxation:
a little alliteration,
and some onomatopoeia
with sonnets and haiku held dear.
Though his verse will always live on
the girl who inspired it has gone.

Tides

She loves to spend time at the beach,
where her troubles seem out of reach.
The woman finds her mind drifting
whenever she feels sand shifting
beneath her feet. Such a relief
to realise that time is brief.
The tide going in and out shows
no awareness of Helen's toes;
Nagging doubts diminish, so small
until nothing matters at all.

Percychatteybooks

Story Telling (R)

Somerset House

6070 Birmingham Business Park

Birmingham

B37 7BF

Registered Number 2299335

Produced and published in the Hondon Valley,
Southern Spain

www.ingramcontent.com/pod-product-compliance
Lightning Source LLC
Chambersburg PA
CBHW060632130626
46555CB00002B/764

* 9 7 8 1 8 3 8 1 2 0 1 0 8 *